Spookier Than a Ghost

by Karen Gray Ruelle

SCHOLASTIC INC.

New York   Toronto   London   Auckland   Sydney
Mexico City   New Delhi   Hong Kong   Buenos Aires

ISBN 0-439-45089-6

12 11 10 9 8 7 6 5 4 3 2 1   2 3 4 5 6 7/0

Printed in the U.S.A.   23

First Scholastic printing, September 2002

Contents

Something Spooky

"My favorite part
   of Halloween is treats,"
   said Harry to his little sister, Emily.
   It was the first day of October.
   Halloween was in thirty days.
   But Harry liked to think ahead.
"I like treats, too," said Emily.
"But the costumes are the best part
   of Halloween," she said.

"What are you going to be?"
  Harry asked Emily.
"Guess!" said Emily.
"A ghost?" said Harry.
"Like last year?"
"No. Something spookier,"
  said Emily.

The year before that,
Harry had been a pirate
and Emily had been a butterfly.
"A butterfly?" said Harry.
"No. Something prettier," said Emily.

The year before that,
Harry had been a tree.
Emily had been too little for
trick-or-treating.
Their mother and father
had dressed her up as a pumpkin.

"A pumpkin?" said Harry.

"No. Something bigger," said Emily.

"A tree?" said Harry.

"No. Even bigger than a tree,"
  said Emily.

"Something spookier than a ghost,
  prettier than a butterfly,
  and bigger than a tree," said Harry.

"I wonder what that can be," he said.

"It will be a surprise!" said Emily.

Jack-o'-Lanterns

There was a lot to do.

Halloween was only two weeks away.

Harry's mother made

Halloween cookies.

She put them in the freezer.

They were for trick-or-treaters.

She also bought little boxes of raisins.

She bought lollipops.

Harry and Emily helped get ready.

They made little paper ghosts.

Then they taped the ghosts

over the lollipops.

Harry's father drew spooky pictures.

Harry and Emily helped.

They cut out bats.

They put the pictures

and bats in the windows.

Harry and Emily drew
faces on pumpkins.
Their mother cut off the tops.
Harry and Emily scooped out
the pumpkin goop.
They scooped out the seeds.

Their father carved the faces.

He got out short, fat candles.

He put them inside the pumpkins.

That made them into jack-o'-lanterns.

Almost everything was ready
for Halloween.

Almost everything.

"What are you wearing for Halloween?"
Harry's mother asked.

"I might be a ghost or a pirate,"
Harry said.

"You were a ghost last year,"
said his mother.

"You were a pirate the year before."

"You could be a ghost pirate,"
said Emily.

Harry thought.

"I know!" he said.

"I want to be a dinosaur."

"What about you, Emily?"
said their mother.

"I can't tell you," said Emily.

"It's a surprise."

"Oh," said their mother.

"Well, if you need any help
   with your costumes,
      ask me," she said.

"Oh, I do not need help," said Emily.

A Dinosaur

It was not easy to make
a dinosaur costume.
First Harry put on
dinosaur-colored clothes.
But it did not look right.

Then he wrapped himself
in a dinosaur blanket.
That did not work, either.
"Are you a dinosaur taking a nap?"
  asked Emily.
"My costume will be
  much better than that," she said.
"Tell me what it is," said Harry.
"I can't," said Emily.

Harry decided to make

a paper costume.

He got a big roll of paper.

He drew the outline

of a big dinosaur.

Then he drew another

one the same size.

He cut them out and painted them.

When the paint was dry,
he taped them together.
He put them on.
He looked like
a dinosaur
with a
Harry head.

"I have an idea for a head,"

said Emily.

She got a large paper bag.

They painted a dinosaur face on it.

They cut out eye holes.

Harry put it on.

Now he looked like a dinosaur.

"This is a great costume!"

said Harry. "Thank you, Emily."

He practiced making dinosaur noises.

Emily went to her room.

She brought a sheet,

a roll of paper, cardboard,

and string.

She brought paint, tape, glue,

and tin foil.

She brought pipe cleaners

and chopsticks.

She was in her room

all day.

She did not

even come

out for

a snack.

Trick-or-Treat

Everything was ready for Halloween.

The pictures and bats

were in the windows.

The jack-o'-lanterns were lit.

All the treats were ready.

Harry went upstairs.

He put on his dinosaur costume.

Emily went upstairs.

She put on her surprise costume.

Harry came down first.

"Hurry up, Emily," he said.

"It's time to trick-or-treat."

Emily came slowly down the stairs.

She was wearing a white sheet.

She had beautiful wings.

She had pumpkin faces on her feet.

She had a crown of leaves.

And she was crying.

"Emily," said Harry.

"What is the matter?"

She sat down on the floor.

She sobbed.

"I tried to make a spooky costume.

I tried to make a beautiful costume.

I tried to make a big costume.

I tried to make a surprise costume.

But all I made was a dumb costume."

Emily sobbed and sobbed.

"But it is beautiful," said Harry.

"It is spooky, too," he said.

"And it makes you look so big,"

he said.

"No one has ever made a costume
like that before," said Harry.
Emily stopped crying.
"And I can tell what you are.
You are a spooky, beautiful,
giant butterfly ghost.
You have landed on a tree
in a pumpkin patch."

Emily smiled a little smile.

Harry helped her up.

"Now let's go trick-or-treating!"

he said.

They each took a Halloween cookie.

They took a box of raisins

and a ghost lollipop.

Now their Halloween bags

would not start out empty.

Then they went out to trick-or-treat.

At every door,

people looked at Emily.

They asked about her costume.

Harry the dinosaur explained.
"She is a spooky, beautiful,
giant butterfly ghost.
She landed on a tree
in a pumpkin patch."
At every door,
Emily got an extra treat.

When they got home,
her bag was full.
It was twice as full as Harry's.
She added her treats to Harry's treats.
The pile was almost big enough
to last them both
until the next Halloween.